Pragmatic Princess

26 Superb Stories of Self-Sufficiency

Written by
Rachel Kowert, PhD

Illustrated by
Randall Hampton

Copyright © 2019 Your Own Castle, LLC
Library of Congress Control Number: 2019915366
All rights reserved

ISBN 978-0-578-58369-3

Production Management by Four Colour Printing
Production Date: October 2019
Printed in the USA

For Zoe, Jude, and Rhys
-RK

For Jonah, Ellie, and Caleb
-RH

To the readers of this book: Remember that your happily ever after is not dependent on magic, or luck, or a knight in shining armor ...you can build your own castle.

Table of Contents

Ava the Adventurous

Ava dreamed of adventures far from Cloud Canyon,
Of exploring the world with her pug companion.
She yearned to travel and to see countries afar,
To learn all about brave Vikings and noble czars.

"This town is simply too boring for me,"
Ava would say, looking toward the sea.
She pondered the ways to see the whole globe,
Airplane, train, car, mini bus, and space probe.

Then she devised an ingenious plan,
How to explore far from her town's dry land.

She realized if she learned more about boating,
Then she would be able to see it by floating.
"To the library!", Ava said, feet to the ground,
"I must learn how to raise the sails up and splash down!"

Once she learned all she could about sailing,
She brushed up on hammering and nailing.
For if Ava was to sail far from home,
She'd need a sturdy sailboat of her own.

So she made a list of all it would take,
For her to sail in the ocean's strong wake.

Next, Ava headed to the hardware store,
She checked her list: glue, a saw, and an oar.
Then she made her way to the fabric shop,
To find something nice for the sail on top.

Ava's last stop was the corner market,
She couldn't set sail without full pockets!
She bought lollipops and some other sweets:
Gummy bears, butterscotch, and chocolate treats.

Ava headed home to nail, saw, and chop.
She set up her tools in her dad's workshop.
She hammered and glued all throughout the night,
To make sure her sailboat was built just right.

Before too long she was ready to sail,
She took care of every single detail.
But Ava first needed to test her boat,
Before fetching her dog to sail afloat.

When she stepped onto her floating raft in the sea,
She was horrified. "Oh no! It fits only me!"

So right back in to the town Ava went,
To expand her boat two hundred percent!
She quickly devised a new improved plan,
And returned to where her shopping began.

On the way though, Ava was taken by surprise,
By the sights around her, they led her to surmise,
That it wasn't supplies that needed to be found,
But rather appreciation for what's around.

18

Parasols from Japan were the first thing she saw,
Then windows of fresh-made croissants and baklava.
Down the road she saw a shop full of German crafts,
Intricate cuckoo clocks and hand-carved wood carafes.

Having always been in such a hurry to leave,
Ava never realized that she could achieve.
Far away adventures right here in her hometown,
They were everywhere, she just had to look around.

Ava knew she would build her great big boat one day,
And be able to sail to cities far away.
But she had learned adventures can be far or near,
Even in her own town, the world was all right here!

All Ava had to do was look around,
There was plenty of adventure to be found.
Before her, the world to explore in Cloud Canyon,
Together with her favorite pug companion.

19

Bella the Brave

Magazines were Bella's favorite book,
She had them stashed everywhere you could look.
They were stacked from the ceiling to the floor,
But still Bella wanted to collect more.

She loved the cover photographs the most,
She stuck them on every wall she could post.
Everyone in Bella's family knew,
That she longed to be in the pictures too.

If you asked Bella, her most perfect day,
Would be with a photo shoot far away.
She'd put on a dress, they'd ask for a snap,
All whilst a circle of onlookers clapped.

She longed for the day she would realize her dream,
Front and center on her favorite magazine.

23

One day at school, Bella brought magazines to share.
She went with her head held high, but left in despair.
For when she said, "One day I'll be in the pictures,"
The classroom became filled with snickers and whispers.

"You don't look anything like those girls there..."
Said the boy in the back with the dark hair.
"Have you seen someone like her up in lights?"
Bella could hear from the girl wearing tights.

$$\begin{array}{cccc} 3 & 7 & 15 & 6 \\ +4 & -6 & +3 & -4 \end{array}$$

$$\begin{array}{cccc} 8 & 4 & 12 & 17 \\ +12 & +7 & -6 & -8 \end{array}$$

Bella ran, magazines scattered all around her,
But her cries could not drown out the sounds of laughter.
It seemed that not one of the children in her class,
Shared Bella's belief that her dream would come to pass.

25

When she got home, Bella ran over to her mom,
And told her she wanted all the magazines gone.
Bella ripped every picture as she tore it down,
Then taking deep breaths, she calmed herself and sat down.

Bella spoke softly from the middle of the fray,
"Mom, something really terrible happened today.
My friends pointed, laughed, and said I would never be
On the cover of any fashion magazine."

"I'm not the right shape, I haven't got the right hair,
They said I don't belong with the models in there."
Bella's mom took her daughters hand and said, "Oh, dear,
They have got it all wrong. Come, have a look right here."

Bella's mom grabbed something from under the staircase,
A book filled with pictures of every shape and face.
There were people of all types: short, tall, round, oblong,
Fair and dark skinned, bald, brunette, red-head, grey, and blonde.

"You see," she said, "everyone has beauty to share,
No matter if you're shaped like a square or a pear."

Bella's face lit up with delight,
She knew that her mother was right.
The kids at school had it all wrong,
Her kind of beauty did belong.

Bella returned to school, head held high from the ground.
She told everyone about the book she had found.
She taught her friends that beauty is in everyone,
No matter what you look like or where you come from.

Christina the Curious

Christina questioned everything under the sun,
She would ask about anything to anyone.
Why was morning sky light but the nighttime sky dark?
How come the happiest birdsongs come from the lark?

What colors are mixed to make grey?
Why do horses neigh and not bray?
Do you know who invented string?
Who, what, why, when, how... everything!

Her hunger for answers could not be abated,
But without strong evidence, would be debated.
"I have heard that penguins waddle but do not fly,
Can we go to the zoo so I can find out why?"

Christina's questions were welcome in the classroom.
They were change of pace from, "Where is the bathroom?"
But sometimes Christina would make quite odd requests.
Just last week, she asked if she could see a skunk nest!

One day her friend Ruby approached her after lunch,
To ask, "Don't you think your questions are a bit much?
Why must you always know how, who, what, why, and where?
Why must you always know? Why do you always care?"

Christina's thoughts came flooding in with a fury,
How could she explain scientific inquiry?
"You mean you don't want to know why the sun shines bright?
Or why helicopters and airplanes can take flight?"

"Not really", Ruby replied with a sigh.
"I just want the school day to hurry by.
I do not need an elaboration,
For every scientific citation."

Christina continued, "My barrage of questions,
Only comes from the very best of intentions.
Without questions or answers we'd never know why,
The sun burns hot, or how planes with propellers fly."

"We'd always wonder why motorcycles are loud,
How stars twinkle at night and what is in a cloud."
Then, looking at Ruby, she had an idea,
For a schoolyard scientific panacea.

"Ruby," she started, "you don't want to take the word,
Of others telling you what they have overheard.
Asking questions and seeing for yourself," she smirked,
"Is the only way to know how and why things work."

"Off to the playground!" was Christina's suggestion,
"To show you the importance of asking questions."

"My brother told me owls sleep upside down,
In pairs, snuggled together, underground.
But that is wrong," she said as she pointed,
As Ruby looked she seemed disappointed.

"You see there? Owls sleep right side up in trees,
Just like all the other birds you can see.
Without questions I would have never known,
That many owls do sleep all on their own."

34

Ruby nodded and seemed to understand,
How important it was to see firsthand.
She realized her friend's questions weren't just quirks,
But the key to knowing how the world works!

Later, when Christina asked about causation,
Ruby smirked quietly in anticipation,
She understood now that questions lead to answers,
Or as Christina would say, "knowledge advancers."

Danielle the Daring

What many others found scary,
Intimidating and wary,
Made Danielle very excited,
Thrilled, charged up, and delighted.

If it was daring, Danielle would give it a go.
She'd already gone swimming with dolphins, you know.
She'd ridden a unicycle, pogo sticks too,
But there was so much more Danielle wanted to do.

One day in town Danielle saw a flyer,
Next to a broken laundromat dryer.
It advertised a motorcycle race,
The prize? A trophy as big as her face!

"That looks like fun," Danielle said with a smile,
"I'm sure I could learn how to ride freestyle."
After grabbing the flyer, off she went,
To get prepared for the racing event.

First stop was the bookstore; she told the clerk,
"I want to know how motorcycles work.
I need to learn how to ride really fast,
When I'm racing, I don't want to be last!"

READ!

Then, it was time to look for her new ride.
What luck! There was one sitting just outside,
Next to the bookstore, with "FREE" on the seat,
"With this bike," Danielle thought "I can't be beat!"

FREE

Over the summer, Danielle practiced day and night,
She mastered hills, jumps, and turning, both left and right.

40

By the day of the race, she felt ready,
Her feet were to the pedals, hands steady.
5, 4, 3, 2, 1, GO! The race started.
The riders took off, and Danielle darted.

She could clearly hear all her friends cheering,
But she remained focused on her steering.
Soon, Danielle passed the racers one by one,
"Whahooooo!" she shouted, "this is so much fun!"

Her adrenaline spiked as she made the first turn,
Up and over a large jump, Danielle's engine churned.
She naviaged through some obstacles - one, two,
Then saw the finish, down the straightaway she flew.

41

All of a sudden, a yellow jersey flew by,
The sound of her engine caught Danielle by surprise.
She flew down the home stretch and beat her to the line,
Danielle crossed behind yellow jersey, #9.

Danielle came to a halt at the roar of the crowd,
And stood tall with the other racers, feeling proud.
Even though she didn't win the trophy and fame,
Danielle knew that she was a winner just the same.

Because she dared to try something brand new,
And she didn't just race the track - she flew!
Danielle was confident she did her best,
Her competition was very impressed.

42

As a new rider, she came in second.
"That's never happened," #9 beckoned.
She leaned in towards Danielle, patting her back,
"I can't believe you are new to this track!"

Danielle was not upset finishing number two,
Because she knew that her riding confidence grew.
Her wish to be daring was now even stronger,
"Next time," she thought, "I'll race a track even longer."

43

Eliana the Energetic

Eliana didn't walk, she zoomed everywhere,
The smoke left behind was how you knew she'd been there.
She was often too busy for a look around,
Because she was bouncing here, there, all through the town.

One day, an old woman stopped her to have a chat,
Under the guise of asking about her new hat.
"Excuse me dear, do you have a minute to spare?
What do you think of my hat - has it enough flair?"

Eliana came to a screeching halt,
And took a long look up from the asphalt.
The woman had a blue and white striped hat,
It was out of shape and slumped to the back.

47

"It is lovely," Eliana said with a smile,
"It's a little smushy, but has a lot of style,
Perhaps prop it up; the wind is really blowing,
Now if you'll please excuse me, I must be going."

"Wait, wait," the old woman pleaded,
"There's something else that I needed.
Energetic Eliana, your friends call you,
What is your secret? Perhaps you can share
a clue?"

"Lately, I've been feeling dragged down,
Like I have a permanent frown.
I only mope, nothing to do,
I just sit around, scowl, and stew."

"I want to stop feeling tired and mad,
And be more like you - energized and glad.
Your positive energy, where's it from?
You are always zooming and rarely glum."

48

Eliana thought, "Not glum? Always on the go?"
Then said to the woman, "I honestly don't know!
I have always preferred moving to standing by,
And do my best to see all things from the bright side.

I think the secret is all about the spirit,
Or whatever it is we choose to bring to it.
Rather than wait for fun, I choose to seek it out,
And I let most things go rather than sit and pout.

Because when we are still, all we can do is see,
But when we choose to move, we can do what we please.
Why wait for adventures when they are to be found?
Why choose to stay mad and let the anger compound?"

49

The old woman laughed, then started to speak,
"Oh my dear, you've been a pleasure to meet.
You are right - that when we seek, we shall find,
Thank you for stopping, you have been so kind."

The woman smiled and set off with a newfound hop.
As she left, she fastened her hat tightly on top.
Eliana started to leave, but hit the brakes,
Then said, "Seek out the bright side; that is all it takes!

Focus on the good in others and every day,
Don't let anyone ever take your joy away.
Just make the best of it all," Eliana grinned,
"When choosing positivity, everyone wins."

Eliana had taught the woman something new,
That positivity was something to pursue.
It won't happen without having actively tried,
Putting forth effort, determination applied.

Eliana also learned something new that day,
An important lesson for her to take away.
She had learned that her energy was contagious,
And sharing it with others was advantageous.
Positivity was a treasure to be shared,
"I must chat more often," Eliana declared.

Eliana still zoomed so fast that the world blurred,
But now stopped on occasion to help spread the word.
"Keep it moving!" she'd say to those still on the ground,
"The best things in life don't happen waiting around!"

Farah the Festive

Farah loved to celebrate everyone's birthday,
Holidays, carnivals, and neighborhood soirees.
She loved the food, music, and the decorations,
Farah would wait for them in anticipation.

Farah's very own birthday was coming up soon.
She dreamt of a huge party with lots of balloons.
Farah thought, "I could pitch a tent right by the bay,
Maybe I could get my favorite band to play.

I could have swings swung by monkeys and ducks on boats,
I wonder if I can find some big flower floats?
We'll have dancers, jugglers, and glitter confetti,
I can't wait for the day to be here already!"

When she told her parents about her plan,
"We are just not sure," their response began,
"We cannot have a big party this year.
We really didn't plan for it, I'm sorry dear."

Even though their final answer was unspoken,
Farah's eyes welled, she felt completely heartbroken.
"But Mom and Dad," Farah said, "parties are the best!
The music and singing, dancing, and all the rest."

"We're not saying you can't have a party at all,
Just a party at home, rather than a grand ball.
No monkeys or ducks, giant flower floats or clowns,
Just some balloons and punch in our backyard playground."

Farah looked at her parents and said with a grin,
"It will be the best party there has ever been!
I will make some bunting and invite the whole school,
We'll have banners, and streamers. It will be so cool!"

HAPPY Birthday

"There's no time to waste," she said with a smirk,
Then, she made a banner out of patchwork.
She sewed the words "HAPPY BIRTHDAY" on top,
It turned out great, the colors really popped.

Then, she made bunting with every crayon color,
And bright paper flowers, both bigger and smaller.
She decorated her whole house, worked very hard,
And even picked up instruments from the junkyard.

A rusty trombone, old guitar, and bent snare drum,
She had recruited a neighborhood band to strum.

It would be the best party Farah ever threw.
She couldn't wait to invite everyone she knew.

Finally, it arrived: Farah's birthday.
The band came early to set up and play.
As she waited for the guests to arrive,
The band started playing a funky jive.

The house filled up quickly with family and friends.
They all loved the decorations of odds and ends.
The place roared with music, laughs, smiles, and cheers,
Farah's party was the best one in years.

58

As they sang "Happy Birthday," Farah's eyes went wide,
As she realized that it's the people inside,
Who make it a party, not a banner above,
Parties are festive when you are with those you love.

The next year, Farah didn't go venue hunting,
But instead rolled out her colored handmade bunting.
Year after year, she hosted her parties at home,
With her close friends, family, and rusted trombone.

Gina the Generous

Giving to others is what Gina found most fun,
Her time, toys, and snacks - sharing them with everyone.

"Pet stuck in a tree? I'll be right over."
"Are you hungry? Here - take my leftovers!"
"Did you want to talk? I can stay all day."
"Ran out of stickers? Have some from my tray!"

One day, Gina went to her neighborhood deli,
For her favorite peanut butter and jelly.

63

On the way, she saw a small cat under a car,
He looked like he had travelled very, very far.
He was terribly thin and seemed really hungry,
Gina promised to bring him back something yummy.

Then she passed by a lonely-looking boy,
Wearing torn jeans and holding an old toy.
He was quiet and he looked hungry, too.
Gina was unsure of what she could do.

She went into the deli and ordered her meal,
Remembering milk for the cat under the wheel.
Then, Gina told the clerk about the boy out there,
And asked if he had any extra food to spare.

64

"We can't give away food for free," he said.
He filled her order and patted her head.
"He'll be fine," he said, then started to sweep,
"You cannot help every person you meet."

Gina was furious; she knew the clerk was wrong.
There's always room to give, her convictions were strong.
As she turned to leave, in her loudest voice she said,
"We can always help. Generosity will spread!"

Gina passed on her sandwich to the boy outside,
And milk to the cat, who was so happy he cried.

Later on, the quiet boy came to the deli,
To offer his thanks for the sandwich with jelly.
The clerk knew he hadn't earned appreciation,
As the boy continued, "We are on vacation.
I don't know this city and I've lost Mom and Dad,
I'm not sure how to find them." he was very sad.

Just then the small cat passed by the deli window,
The clerk recognized him: his missing cat, Bingo!
He had looked everywhere for him to no avail,
He pet him and noticed something around his tail.

A cup from this very deli, striped white and grey.
He recalled the milk Gina had bought just that day.
Then, he remembered his condescending head pat,
Yet, she'd been generous to the boy and his cat.

66

Gina's generosity taught him a lesson,
That one fateful day at his delicatessen.
Sometimes people (and cats) of all kinds and all sorts,
Might be in need of others' generous support.

The clerk now knew what to do; he picked up the phone,
Found the boy's parents and promised to bring him home.
The clerk then made the boy another plate to eat,
And packed him a to-go box filled up with sweet treats.

From then on, the clerk was more like that little girl,
Who wanted nothing more than to give to the world.
"Channel your inner Gina!" was his policy,
Because nothing can spread like generosity.

67

Harriet the Helpful

Harriet often volunteered for fun,
She enjoyed helping her friends and loved ones.
If you were in need of help with a task,
Harriet would be there, no questions asked!

Just the past week at her school's movie club,
There was a bit of a scheduling flub.
Harriet came to lend a helping hand,
To set up and run the concession stand.

And last night, her dad needed assistance,
With a circuit that lost its resistance.
Harriet to the rescue, tools in hand,
Sleeves rolled and wearing a lighted headband.

With a bit of tinkering, it wasn't too long,
The resistor was resisting and going strong.
Her dad was shocked, but Harriet was not surprised,
As "tasks are easier with extra hands and eyes."

71

This evening, it was her school's yearly costume ball.
This year, they were raising money for a band hall.
Harriet had signed up to be a volunteer,
A "meeter and greeter," as she did every year.

Before long, she noticed some of parents in the back,
Whispering to each other, huddled in a pack.
Harriet moved closer so she could hear them speak,
And heard the tall man call the costume party "bleak."

Another complained, "...and the price of admission!?
What about these long lines? We need a petition!"
Then, the slender woman added, "This isn't right,
This is not how I planned on enjoying my night."

Harriet interrupted their conversation,
To clear up the matter of the situation.

"Excuse me, but I overheard what you were saying,
About the long lines and prices you are paying.
It's because we just don't have enough volunteers,
Perhaps you can be on the committee next year."

"Maybe sign up to become a sponsor,
To help cover the costs of the concert.
Or donate something: chairs, food, or decor?
As you can see, we could use a bit more.
It takes a lot for a party's success,
The more volunteers we have, the less stress!"

The parents were quiet, taken aback,
They didn't know it was helpers they lacked.

The tall man was the first to start speaking,
He stammered a bit but then said meekly,
"Well, perhaps next year I could lend some chairs,
So no one would have to sit on the stairs."

"I own the bakery with the cupcake doormat,"
Chimed in the slender woman in the black veiled hat.
"Next year, I am sure, the bakery could make do,
Donating some cakes and a pastry or two."

"Wonderful," Harriet said with a smile.
"I'm glad I came here to chat for a while.
You know, the more people who get involved,
The easier it is to problem-solve."

74

Next year at the ball, oh! There were plenty of chairs,
And sweets of all shapes: triangles, circles, and squares.
They ended up raising more than ever that year,
All because they had so many more volunteers.

Helping had made it easier to get things done,
Quicker, simpler, and (of course) way more fun.
Harriet kept on helping in every way,
She knew no better way to spend the day.

Isabel the Incredible

Isabel was not like the other girls,
She wasn't excited by frills and pearls.
While her friends enjoyed dancing and twirling,
She spent her time studying and learning.

Isabel's grandma was a famous magician,
Giuliana the Grand, she earned top commission!
People travelled far and wide to see her perform,
Her shows always sold out, even in a snowstorm.

Isabel knew there was the possibility,
She could hone her own magical ability.
Once a week, for as long as she could remember,
Isabel and her grandma studied together.
With every new lesson, Isabel's talents grew,
She kept it a secret, and made sure no one knew.

79

One day, she was ready for her skills to be shown,
To prove to herself how much her magic had grown.
So she signed up for a talent competition,
After obtaining her grandmother's permission.

When the day of the talent show arrived,
The entire town seemed to come alive.
All of Cloud Canyon had come to the show,
Even though it had just started to snow.

Before too long, it was Isabel's turn,
She could feel her stomach nervously churn.

She took a deep breath and straightened her coat,
Propped up her top hat and then cleared her throat.
Then she checked her sign, lifting up her head,
"Isabel the Incredible," it read.

80

Isabel was the last one to perform that day.
Once she hit the stage, she just took it away!
She reached down in her top hat and out came rabbit ears.
Isabel pulled off her magic to claps and cheers.

Isabel's magic show was quite a sight.
She took home the largest trophy that night.

After the show, she overheard backstage,
A woman standing by the rabbit cage.
"I really thought the winning act was grand,
But magic is only just sleight of hand."

Isabel turned toward the offender.
"Excuse me, but I am no pretender.
I know that the rabbit came from a cage,
But magic is real," she said in a rage.

81

Isabel grabbed a deck of cards from her pocket,
And on one asked the woman to draw a rocket.
Then, she returned it to the top of the pile,
And Isabel shuffled the deck for a while.

Isabel looked at the woman right straight in the eye,
And asked her if she could see her card in the sky.
Confused, the woman looked up to see a flurry,
Of cards in the air, everything was all blurry.

As the cards fell slowly down to the floor,
Isabel heard a collective uproar.
Stuck on the ceiling was the teacher's card,
The truth she could no longer disregard.
Magic was real, she could plainly see,
As she stared at her card, spade number three.

The woman's mouth fell open wide in awe,
She could not be sure of what she just saw.
Isabel truly was a magician,
Carrying on her family tradition.

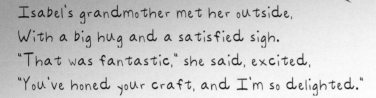

Isabel's grandmother met her outside,
With a big hug and a satisfied sigh.
"That was fantastic," she said, excited,
"You've honed your craft, and I'm so delighted."

Isabel was proud of her family tradition,
And she never lost her magical ambition.
She'd surely keep her family history alive,
With her card and hat tricks, and
grandma by her side.

Jasmine the Just

Jasmine the Just had the most unique flair:
Making sure all the decisions were fair.
Equity was the most important thing,
That is, to evenly share everything.

At lunch one day, Jasmine heard some clatter,
And looked up to see what was the matter.
There was cake in the school lunchroom that day,
And the last piece of it was causing quite a fray. 87

"The last piece is mine!," Farah shrieked,
"No, it's not!" Isabel's voice peaked.
"I didn't get one! Don't you care?"
"I didn't either! That's not fair!"

In an effort to help them find a truce,
Jasmine offered a solution to use:
"Why don't you simply cut the piece in half?"
The answer was so easy, they all laughed.

Then Jasmine cut the piece of cake,
But that caused another small quake.
The pieces were not exactly the same,
they began fighting over which to claim.

"Stop it, please!" Jasmine's voice interjected,
"This is not at all what I expected.
One piece might be bigger than the other,
But that's no reason to fight. Oh brother!"

Jasmine examined the situation,
So she could prevent more altercations.
Because, for Jasmine, it simply must be,
That everybody be treated justly.

One piece did look a bit bigger,
But the other had more rigor.
Extra frosting and fewer crumbs,
They were as even as they come.

Then Jasmine thought about what the girls were saying,
And concluded it was foolish, their dismaying.
They were fighting over something that was a treat,
A luxury, bonus, an extra special sweet.

89

"You know," Jasmine continued on,
"I think that we have it all wrong."

"We should only be looking at another's plate,
To make sure that everything about it looks great.
Just to check that everyone has enough to eat,
Not for comparing the portion size of your treat.

You know, fair doesn't always equate to equal,
Fair sometimes means different things to different people.
For me, it's everyone in our communities,
Getting the same chances and opportunities."

Jasmine left her friends and sat to finish her food,
While the girls agreed they had the wrong attitude.
Jasmine had helped them to solve their lunchroom treat brawl,
They sat down with gratitude they had cake at all.

Jasmine continued to negotiate,
Anytime there was a classroom debate.
But the next time she witnessed a fight about food,
She had one person cut, and the other one choose.

Kristen the Kind

When Kristen headed out for school,
Her mom sent her off with a rule:

"Be kind to everyone you see,
Kindness costs nothing - it is free.
And be friends with everyone you will meet,
Because you never know who you might greet."

Kristen always followed her mom's advice,
To extend kindness and always be nice.
She would open doors for those with full hands,
And give encouragement to sidewalk bands.

At snack time, she always shared her crackers,
Even the chocolate ones in blue wrappers.
Kirsten always kept extra treats around,
In case there was a stray pet to be found.

And when she heard others complain,
About the long lines, their friends, or the rain,
Kristen didn't get discouraged,
For she knew kindness took courage.

One day at recess, she saw a girl on the side,
Sitting alone on a bench behind the big slide.
Kristen walked over and sat down close beside her,
Said hello and asked if something was the matter.
Kristen didn't know her, but she started talking,
Mumbling softly, while looking down at her stockings.

"I, uh... my family just moved to this town,
My name is Jasmine," she said with a frown.
"It's my first day and I don't know whether,
Anyone will want to play together?"

97

"I will play with you," Kristen responded.
Jasmine grinned, and they instantly bonded.
"I'm sure it's hard being new," she went on,
"Yes," replied Jasmine, "my friends are all gone."

"Well Cloud Canyon is so nice," Kristen chatted,
"The school is full of fun kids," she added.
"I'm sure you will make loads of new friends here,
You don't need to worry too much, my dear.
How about this? I'll be your first new friend!
Let's play together until recess ends!"

Then, Kristen pointed to a pile of leaves,
"Want to jump in there with me? Puh-leee-ease?
The other girls don't like to get dirt on their clothes,
What else is there to do during recess? Who knows!?"

The girls ran to the biggest pile they'd ever seen,
The leaves were so colorful: yellow, red, bright green.
Together, they leaped in with no passivity,
It quickly became their favorite activity.

Starting from that day when the girls first met,
There were no two better friends, you could bet.
They became the best friends that friends could be,
One without the other, you'd never see.

Kristen was grateful for her mom's guidance,
And her rules about friendship and kindness.
Without them, Kristen may not have ever,
Met her new best friend, and played together.

Lina the Leader

Lina was surely the most eloquent speaker,
Some would say she was a natural born leader.
Head of the quiz bowl, speech club, and the debate team,
Class president - Lina lead everything it seemed.

Last month, Lina's school announced a competition,
For the debate team; Lina had high ambition.
For weeks, she had been coaching her entire team,
In mock debates, ranging from the odd to mainstream.

Chocolate or vanilla ice cream, which is the best?
What is the ideal morning time to get dressed?
Will humans ever colonize Mars, yes or no?
What's the best way to make my mom's hydrangeas grow?

Week after week, they practiced debating,
Challenging, questioning, advocating.
Finally, they felt ready to compete,
And were confident they would not be beat.

At last, the big competition arrived,
The main debate question had been contrived.
How should their school spend their extra money;
Invest more in math or social studies?

Lina and her team were asked to go first,
Their argument was practiced and well versed.
"The math department needs the investment,
As they are the root of all assessments."

"Without math we couldn't keep score,
Make some change or measure a door.
No question, they should certainly get the cash,"
Lina's team argued with panache.

Then the team from the neighboring school had their turn,
A boy stepped up to the podium, looking stern.
He began stating that he thought everyone knew,
Investments in social studies were overdue.

"Social studies are key for our communities,
to promote cooperation and unity.
While math is, of course, an important subject too,
It is not more so than 'me' understanding 'you'."

The judges seemed to deliberate for ages,
Then, a judge stepped forward holding several pages.
They concluded that they couldn't collectively,
Decide which team had argued most effectively.

A tie in debate had never happened before,
"How do we break the tie?" both of the teams implored.

The judges devised a new tiebreaker.
Each team would nominate a debater,
To support the other team's position,
Of which department earned an addition.

The team quickly turned to Lina for direction,
They hadn't prepared for additional questions.
Christina whispered, "Argue the opposing side?
Is this really the only way to break the tie?"

The teams were given minimal time to confer,
Lina knew that her team was relying on her.
She took the stage across from her competitor,
Mind racing but composed, she faced the questioner.

"Social studies are very important to learn,
To increase community and social concern.
While we strongly argued that math is essential,
Social studies are key to human potential.
When we learn about other people and places,
Foreign traditions and customs, other races,
We begin to foster our sense of charity,
Aand set roots for the cornerstones of empathy."

The boy was stunned as he looked Lina in the eyes,
He was silent; a new stance he could not surmise.
He was taken aback by Lina's rebuttal,
And did not even try mustering a mumble.

Lina's team had won the debate,
Because of their hard work, not fate.
Through practice, Lina had increased her competence,
To meet the tie-breaking challenge with confidence.

She was proud to have made school debate history,
Leading the first ever tie-breaking victory.

In the end, the prize money went to the school band,
For a new concert hall complete with a grandstand.
Though, the next year there were two beneficiaries,
Math and social studies, thanks to their victory.

Marisol cherished capturing the everyday,
The brief moments that can easily fade away.
The morning sun, a silly smile, a good-bye hug,
A lucky chance encounter with a friendly pug.

She wanted to remember each moment,
To capture every daily component.
So she began photographing it all:
Her friends, her family, the school's masked ball.

An abandoned shoe string on a wire,
A stack of old motorcycle tires.
A grandma's sweet smile, a tearful good-bye,
A bakery full of freshly baked pies.

Marisol liked ordinary moments the best,
"Why only capture big events, but not the rest?"

One day, Marisol was taking pictures,
Of some girls in gym class trading whispers,
When the gym coach tapped her on the shoulder,
Marisol thought she was there to scold her.

"Marisol, why are you always behind the lens?
Shouldn't you be over there playing with your friends?"
The coach sighed and shook her head in disapproval,
"Spending time with your friends at this age is crucial."

"But coach, if I put it down, I might miss something!
Just earlier today, Bella was on the swing.
It was the perfect weather, the wind in her hair,
That moment would be lost if I hadn't been there."

112

The coach thought about what Marisol said,
And smiled slightly before nodding her head.
"It is nice that you captured that moment,
But not if it ruins your enjoyment.
You'll miss out if you are always ten feet away,
Let's put the camera down for the rest of day."

Marisol sighed, but handed it over.
She then joined some friends playing red rover.
She soon had forgotten about the need,
To capture every brief smile and good deed.

The day passed faster than she remembered,
She missed out on nothing whatsoever.
Marisol enjoyed every moment with her friends,
Together they laughed, danced around, and played pretend.

At the end of the day, she returned to the gym,
To retrieve the camera she gave up on a whim.

"Well," the coach smiled, "Did you have a good day?"
"It was fantastic!" she began to say.
"I played with my friends, we swung on the swings,
And I didn't miss out on anything."

The coach started laughing, Marisol giggled too,
They were equally proud of her recent breakthrough.
"Now don't lose your passion," the coach said with a smile,
"Just stay on this side of the lens once in a while."

Marisol still captured the moments of the day:
A high five, a traffic jam, a pretty archway.
But she had learned not to fear missing a moment,
As both sides of the camera lens are important.
She would always want to capture the morning dew,
But having fun with her friends was important too.

Noa the Neat

Noa liked everything in its very own place,
Notebooks sorted by color, pencils in a case.
"An organized room leads to an organized day,"
Is what Noa's friends regularly heard her say.

One day, Noa was off looking for adventure,
With her friend Ava; they were digging for treasure.
Ava suggested searching by the old tunnel,
But first going by her house to get some shovels.

When they got to the house and entered Ava's room,
Noa was taken aback - everything was strewn!
She knew they couldn't find a shovel in this mess,
Because where to start looking was anyone's guess.

120

After an hour of digging, Noa stated,
"Maybe it's better if the treasure hunt waited."
"We could clean up your room instead?" she suggested,
"Maybe..." Ava muttered. "It has been neglected."

There were piles of books all over the floor,
Paper flying out of every desk drawer.
Ava said, "It could be a bit neater,
There is something on every square meter!"

Noa nodded as she straightened her composure,
Before giving Ava's room a good once-over.
Books stacked upside-down? An unfinished game of chess?
Is that a boat?! Ava's room was a total mess.

The girls began picking everything up,
Shoes, glasses, magazines, plates, and teacups.
Baskets and buggies... a rotary wing?
Ava must have had one of everything!

121

"What you need is a little organization,
So looking for things doesn't end in frustration."
"When each and everything has its own little niche,
Then you can go about your day without a hitch!"

After hours of picking, sifting and sorting,
And a brief lecture on the perils of hoarding,
Ava and Noa took in all of their hard work,
Everything was now in its own place. Ava smirked,

122

"Thank you, Noa! This whole room feels brand new,
And I couldn't have done this without you.
Now that everything is ready at hand,
Our adventures will be easy to plan!

I used to think being neat was a chore,
An inconvenience, a bit of a bore.
But now that I can grab my things with ease,
I can go on adventures as I please!"

"Yes!" Noa replied excitedly with a nod,
"Some people think my passion for neatness is odd.
But being able to find things quickly is great,
It especially helps when you are running late!"

The girls went to finish their adventure,
To search and find some lost buried treasure.
They quickly grabbed all the tools they needed,
Shovels, buckets, and hats - list completed!

The girls made their way out the door in seconds flat,
That day, and for every adventure after that.

Any lost item, Ophelia quickly found,
Her observation skills were truly world-renowned.
She must have found over a thousand lost objects,
As she never turned down a lost and found project.

Just last week, she found Danielle's missing keys,
Which she had misplaced in a grove of trees.
And when Yuna's dog ran off in the park,
Ophelia got him home before dark.

She had found every single lost barrette,
Notecard and shoe, glasses, jacket and pet.
With the exception of one unsolved case:
Bingo, the tabby cat, remained displaced.

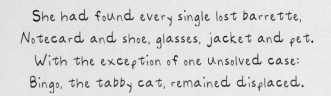

Bingo had been missing for quite a while,
He was last seen strolling the deli aisles.
For weeks, Bingo's owner had been upset,
Hoping Ophelia would find his lost pet.

But Ophelia didn't have new connections,
Leads to follow or neighborly recollections.
It was like Bingo disappeared into thin air,
But Ophelia knew he had to be somewhere.

One day, when Ophelia had left the deli,
To question people she had questioned already,
She noticed somebody she did not recognize;
A young boy eating a sandwich off to the side.

128

So Ophelia stopped right in front of the store,
And said "Excuse me, I haven't seen you before.
I've been looking everywhere for this missing cat."
She held Bingo's missing poster up to the chap.

"Have you seen him?" she asked; he looked up from the ground,
He hadn't seen the cat that needed to be found.

He shook his head no, while he continued to chew,
And then blurted out, "Wait! Maybe I can help you!"

"I just saw a girl, she was in a fret,
she mentioned something about a lost pet.
She headed over there, down that alley,
In the direction of the green valley."

Soon, she spotted something under a car,
Skinny and furry, with a little scar.
Could it be Bingo? She couldn't be sure,
He looked thinner, older, and more demure.

Then she saw a grey and white paper cup,
The cat was using it to lap milk up.
As Ophelia slowly crept closer,
She knew it was the cat from the poster.

"Bingo, it's you!" Ophelia loudly shouted,
"I knew I would find you, I shouldn't have doubted!"
"Where on Earth have you been traveling? France? Qatar?
It looks like you have been unbelievably far."

Ophelia let Bingo finish drinking up,
Then happily carried him along with his cup.
Together, they made their way back up the alley,
She was so glad to return the missing tabby.

But, as they got closer to their destination,
Bingo must have recalled the deli's location,
Because he jumped down with the cup around his tail,
And ran full speed toward the deli with a soft wail.

Bingo was happy to no longer roam,
Ophelia was happy he was home.
She attributed her observation,
As the key to her investigation.

Without noticing the boy on the street,
The one with the deli sandwich to eat,
She would not have ever successfully retrieved,
The new details that the boy had perceived.

That day, Ophelia retained her perfect score,
Of finding all of the lost objects, pets, and more.
When others asked for her secret, she would reply:
"A good investigation begins with your eyes!"

131

Every morning before school, Paige would go to meet,
A group of children, to help them across the street.
She'd put on a yellow vest, hold a big red sign,
And would make sure that no students were left behind.

One winter morning. Paige woke up to fresh snowfall,
It looked so magical, piling up on the wall.
Peering outside, she didn't want to leave her bed,
To put on boots and mittens, a hat on her head.

Paige stretched her legs, let out a scratchy cough,
The cold weather made her feel a little bit off.
She just wanted to curl up in her sheets,
With a good book and a big bowl of sweets.

From her bed, Paige continued to watch the snow fall,
A bigger snowstorm than this, she could not recall.
But before too long the storm began to subside,
And Paige thought of the kids she was supposed to guide.

It looked so cold outside, and her bed felt so warm,
Paige didn't want to go out in her uniform.
But she knew she was supposed to protect the street,
For the little children, so Paige rose to her feet.

She arrived to children in an array,
Making snowmen, riding sleds, pulling sleighs.
They came early to wait in the courtyard,
to play with their favorite crossing guard.

One child brought donuts that her parents had purchased,
As a thank you to Paige for her daily service.
Another brought hot chocolate with whipped cream on top,
And a third, a box of tissues and some mint cough drops.

Paige received some lovely presents that day,
Including some handmade cards to display,
As a thank you for always following the rules,
And for making sure the kids got safely to school.

137

There was one card which stood out from the stack,
With "Paige the Protector" written in black.
Inside, there was a drawing of Paige like a knight,
With gold armor, riding a horse and smiling bright.
Glitter was used to create a background blizzard,
And a hundred snowflakes had been cut with scissors.

Paige was overwhelmed by the kindness shown that day,
For doing something she loved doing anyway.
She was so glad that the weather, cold and gloomy,
Didn't keep her from carrying out her duties.

138

Before Paige led the little kids off the threshold,
She thanked them for playing together in the cold.
Then stood in front of them all, feeling filled with pride,
And said, "I'm so glad that I didn't stay inside."

"This morning, I wanted to stay in bed all day,
If I did, then I wouldn't have been here to play.
So even though the weather is quite unpleasant,
And the snow inconvenient, I'm here and present.

Remember the importance of following through,
Because keeping your word is the right thing to do.
Be sure to always show up when you say you'll come,
So your responsibilities don't go undone."

Soon, they all started calling Paige "The Protector",
She felt proud that was how they all remembered her;
as someone to count on, even when things are down.
Paige was the official protector of the town!

139

Quinn learned more quickly than anyone else she knew,
She had mastered French by age three, reading by two.
She could paint portraits in every artistic style,
And knew where each thing was in each grocery aisle.

Quinn's quickness was that extra special part,
Which made her unique and set her apart.
Her family thought that it was a delight,
They fought for her for their team on game night.

When Quinn went to school, it was a different story,
Her friends didn't like that she got all the glory.

She won all the math bowls and every spelling bee,
Made the best diorama of Cloud Canyon's sea.
In band, when Quinn - again - made first chair for trombone,
Even the friendliest of kids began to groan.

In a city-wide competition last autumn,
Quinn was the fastest to solve the logic problem.
When she won, she overheard some of her friends say,
"Why bother when Quinn wins everything anyway?"

Quinn did not like hearing the negative feedback,
She started sitting alone at school, in the back.
She stopped asking questions and didn't raise her hand,
She even quit playing in the school's marching band.

Quinn knew that she couldn't help being quick,
New information would always just stick.
It didn't take effort, it was her quirk,
It just happened to be how her mind worked.

One day at recess, Quinn was alone on the ground,
Reading a book and working hard not to be found,
When her friend Kristen ran past, chasing a loose ball,
Which narrowly missed Quinn's head, it was a close call!

"Oops!" Kristen said; she started to head back to play,
But stopped to ask, "Why are you out here anyway?"
Quinn looked up from her book, feeling like an outcast.
"No one likes a know-it-all," Quinn mumbled at last.

Kristen shook her head, knelt down by Quinn, and replied,
"No way! And besides, that's not a reason to hide.
You know, I happen to think you are a treasure,
I love that I am friends with someone so clever!

You know fun facts, and you are a great debater,
And the city's absolute best trombone player.
Don't let other people's opinions bring you down,
I think you're the most interesting girl in town!"

145

Quinn looked up at Kristen, her eyes beaming,
"You really think all that? You're not teasing?"
Kristen laughed, "I think you are a delight!
You'd be my number one choice on game night!"

"People get upset when they have to try harder,
But it's not your fault you are faster and smarter.
In the end, being challenged makes us all better,
And you cannot really know it all, not really ever."

Both girls laughed and Quinn got up from the ground.
Walking back, she thought of something profound:

In life, she might always encounter resistance,
To her extraordinary characteristics.
But, to Quinn, being quick was the centrality,
That defined who she was, her personality.

So she decided to no longer stress,
And to never again try to be less.
What other people thought, did not matter,
It was just frustration, idle chatter.

146

By the end of the year, Quinn had so many wins,
That the school's trophy cupboard was filled to the brim.
Her school friends started to joke that somehow, someway,
Maybe someone would beat her at something, someday.

Never again did Quinn feel bad for being quick,
A history buff or good with a hockey stick.
She knew that her friends liked her just the way she was,
Even if she did always get the most applause.

147

Ruby carried everything imaginable,
In her backpack, the size was unfathomable.
Ribbons of all colors, Band-Aids, a toolbox, toys,
Kazoos, and whistles, and other things that made noise.

Towels and tea, her beloved stuffed turtle,
Sunscreen, flashlights, a dozen felt circles.
Cans of pea soup and a handful of maps,
Large spools of twine and at least thirteen hats.

There were so many bits and bobs in Ruby's pack,
That no one was sure how she kept it on her back.

Everyone was generally understanding,
Of Ruby's imposing bag, ever expanding.
The kids at school concluded that Ruby either,
Was really prepared or an obsessive keeper.

151

No one had said anything, at least to her face,
About Ruby's backpack taking up too much space.
Even though her backpack had started to impair,
The space in the hallways and in between desk
chairs.

Then, one day at the cafeteria buffet,
Ruby heard someone say her bag was in the way.
She had bumped in to a few people, a few times,
It always got in people's ways when forming lines.

"Why does she carry all that stuff around?"
"I swear she is carrying the whole town!"
"I mean, it's a bit bizarre, don't you think?"
"Do you think she carries a kitchen sink?"

Ruby turned around as fast as she could,
To let the girls know they misunderstood.
"I realize you don't share my passion,
But I don't carry this bag for fashion."

152

"Don't you remember the last field trip to the zoo?
When everyone seemingly contracted the flu.
My backpack was the one with tissues, soup, and tea.
We would have been worse without it," the girls agreed.

"And when that science experiment went wonky,
And the teacher fainted, and the air got funky,
I was the one with the escape route in my bag,
That got everyone outside without any lag."

The girls stood, quiet, and then shared a nod,
They were sorry for calling Ruby odd.
They knew Ruby being at the ready,
Was helpful to all of them already.

Ruby went on, "I like to be prepared,
So I don't need to be concerned or scared.
My bag is a bit clunky and awkward, I know,
But I have what we need no matter where we go!"

153

In class that day, the lesson just happened to be,
On how to kindly accept friends and family.
The teacher said, "If you feel you don't understand,
Something or someone, it's best to ask them firsthand.

The next time you feel curious about something,
Go to the person directly without judging.
You'll learn so much more by talking to each other,
Than from hearsay or gossip with one another."

154

As soon as the teacher finished speaking,
All school fire alarms started shrieking.
The whole classroom began to go manic,
The lights flickered off; the teacher panicked.

But not Ruby, she calmly got up from the floor,
Passed out flashlights and got everyone out the door.
The kids were all grateful for Ruby's bag that day,
Because her readiness got them all out okay.

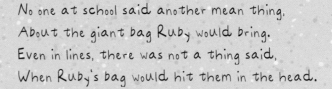

No one at school said another mean thing,
About the giant bag Ruby would bring.
Even in lines, there was not a thing said,
When Ruby's bag would hit them in the head.

Sarah was a typical Cloud Canyon student,
She loved her friends, and wanted to be included.
In their fun weekend activities by the sea,
But got nervous when the group was larger than three.

Isabel and Quinn were Sarah's very best friends,
With whom Sarah frequently played with on the weekends.
But when the group got bigger, it wasn't as fun,
And she would retreat home to a party of one.

159

One day at school, Sarah got an invitation,
To her classmate Farah's birthday celebration.
The guest list was full of people whom Sarah knew,
But still she remained unsure about what to do.

She really did not want to disappoint her friend,
Who was excited about her party weekend.
But Sarah knew that she needed to be earnest,
About how she avoided parties on purpose.

Sarah said, "Your party sounds really great,
But I'm not sure that I can make the date."
Farah sighed, "Aww! But we'll have a big cake,
Music, a magician, and fresh ice cream milkshakes!"

Sarah knew that she had to be sincere,
She admitted, "Parties fill me with fear.
I don't know what to do, or where to stand,
And I never know where to put my hands."

Farah responded, "Thanks you being honest.
I hope you will come, but I know you can't promise."

Sarah could tell that Farah wanted her to go,
So she thought of asking her friends to come in tow.
With Isabel and Quinn close by her side, she thought,
She would feel more comfortable, not as scared or fraught.

But there was a problem with Sarah's plan,
It was done almost before it began.
"We can't go with you," her friends admitted,
"Because we are already committed."

They girls had already prepared an arrangement,
They were to be Farah's party's entertainment.
Isabel was an incredible magician,
And Quinn, Cloud Canyon's best amateur musician.

Quinn offered a new idea, "What about this,
Instead, why don't we ask Harriet to come with?"
"Yes, we should!" Isabel chimed in wholeheartedly.
"Let's ask if she can ride with us to the party."

"We will have to arrive early, you know,
To set up and be ready for our show."

"But if we can arrive all together,"
Sarah said, "I'd feel a whole lot better."

Harriet was on board with the idea too,
Because helping out was her favorite thing to do.
So when the day finally came, they went as a troop,
And arrived early to the party as a group.

62

Quinn played the trombone beautifully that night,
And Isabel's magic was a highlight.
All night, Sarah stayed with Harriet and mingled,
Danced, and laughed and shared a milkshake
with sprinkles.

Even though Sarah didn't like groups of people,
And preferred smaller events that were more
peaceful,
That night, she was able to enjoy a good time,
At a large, loud party with her friends by her side.

Sarah was so glad to have found a way,
To make it to Farah's party that day.
Because Sarah was sincere with her friends,
She had a blast, from beginning to end!!

Best of all, Farah was so excited,
That everyone came who was invited.
That night, the kids of Cloud Canyon had fun,
Even sincere Sarah, party of one.

163

Tabitha always had something to say,
She talked every minute of every day.
She covered every subject possible,
From the dramatic to the comical.

At school she constantly got in trouble,
For talking instead of solving puzzles.
While the teacher was giving instructions,
No one liked the constant interruptions.

Tabitha always had something to share,
A funny joke that she knew from somewhere,
Or sometimes a story that she had heard,
Often the things she said were quite absurd.

Last week, she told an unbelievable story,
About a talking horse that lives in the quarry.
Then, she polled all the children who were in the room,
If they thought yetis were just people in costumes.

There was no pattern to the chatter she'd transmit,
If Tabitha had a thought, she shared it - that's it.

Then, not because of a specific incident,
Her chatter became labeled as an irritant.

Tabitha's jokes during announcements would be shushed,
When she interrupted others, she would be hushed.
Tabitha was confused why her friends would now balk,
At everything she said, anytime she would talk.

One day at school, Tabitha was telling Bella,
About a new book she had bought, a novella.
She could tell Bella wasn't really listening,
Just nodding and smiling; it felt quite distancing.

Tabitha stopped talking and abruptly went mute,
Then Bella looked up and said "That story was cute."
"You were not even listening!" Tabitha fumed,
"Why didn't you look up? I was talking to you!"

"I'm sorry," Bella said, "but you talk a whole lot,
It makes it hard to tell what's important or not.
I am sorry for not listening intently,
I was just trying to be polite and friendly."

169

Bella continued, "You know, it is just,
A person can only listen so much.
Some people seem to share the opinion,
That you only talk, and never listen.

No one likes to feel like they are not heard,
And you really chat away undeterred.
I suspect everyone would be less peeved,
And you would likely be better received,
If you started listening to others;
Your constant talking makes us feel smothered."

170

Tabitha was upset, but told Bella she'd try.
"I don't listen to my friends!?" She felt mortified.
The next day, for every story Tabitha told,
She held her tongue and listened to others threefold.

She learned so much about her friends that day;
That last month, Yuna's dog had run away,
That Noa had helped Ava clean her room,
And that Lina's mom's garden was in bloom.

Tabitha realized listening wasn't a chore,
She felt closer to her friends than ever before.

That day, Tabitha thanked Bella for being brave,
And not brushing her off with a nod and a wave.
While her absurd stories would never cease to shock,
She now understood she should listen, not just to talk.

Everyday Ursula enjoyed going to school,
She got good grades and never broke a single rule.
History was her most favorite subject of all,
She was fascinated by old buildings and halls.

Ursula also had a very unique trait,
Which no one who she met could ever duplicate.
She knew what others said without a hearing a sound,
Her friends thought it was the coolest talent around!

This is because Ursula's audibility,
Had a limited range of capability.
She couldn't hear others when they spoke or made sounds,
But with her unique skills, she was fine in a crowd.

She could read lips to tell what others were saying,
Near or far, she would know what they were conveying.
Her friends would often put her up to a challenge,
Which she always seemed to successfully manage.

She also spoke a whole other language,
Which gave her a pretty cool advantage.
By making shapes and gestures with her hands,
She could share (without words) her daily plans.

Using sign language to clearly communicate,
Was something her friends thought was pretty great.
Because they got to learn sign language too,
Each week there was a new workbook to do.

Everyone welcomed the extra workload,
Because they loved learning her "secret code."

One day, the class was out on a special trip,
To a lighthouse that guided sailing ships.
Ursula was the most excited one,
She knew it was sure to be so much fun.

After a while they arrived to a rocky cliff,
The sea air was salty; Ursula took a whiff.
There were several schools visiting that morning.
The path to the lighthouse was twisting and turning.

The kids of Cloud Canyon headed for the building,
Ursula was the first in the line; it was thrilling.

She had a flurry of questions for her teacher,
About this lighthouse's particular features.
How tall is the lighthouse? Can the owner have pets?
What should you do if you see a boat in distress?

As Ursula started signing her first question,
Everyone heard a girl say, with no discretion,
"What's wrong with that girl there? Is that really her voice?
And what's up with her hands? Does she do that by choice?"

The girl was mocking Ursula's movements,
Making fun of her for pure amusement.

Some began to laugh in Ursula's direction,
So her friend Zoe turned to make a correction:

"Excuse me, but there's nothing wrong with my friend's voice,
Don't you know what someone sounds like isn't their choice?
And talking with her hands, that is our secret code,
Of which the kids in Cloud Canyon have been bestowed.
Do your friends have a code?" The girl was diminished,
"My friend is unique like we all are," she finished.

Zoe nodded and took Ursula's hand with grace,
Then said, "Come on my dear friend, let's check out this place."
They walked up the path together, right to the top,
But just before they reached the peak, Ursula stopped.

As they stood there overlooking the sea,
She asked her friend, "Why were they mean to me?"
Zoe felt unsure about what to say,
She'd never seen someone acting that way.

Zoe thought for a moment, then implored,
"They've never met someone like you before.
People seem the most eager to critique,
The things that make other people unique."

Ursula nodded slowly, but still looked upset,
So Zoe continued, "You should try not to fret.
If I got a coin when someone was mean to me,
We'd all be getting into this lighthouse for free!"

The girls laughed, and then made their way inside,
They toured the lighthouse from top to seaside.

Heading back, they saw the girls from before pass by,
Who mouthed the word "Sorry" before waving goodbye.

Ursula stopped after reading their lips,
and paused for a moment, hands on her hips.
Then approached the girls with a smile and wave,
To show them that they were alike, the same.

"I know I sound different and have to use my hands,
To help others know what I need, to understand.
And I know that others find it odd or unique,
But it is really a super power, I think.

I can watch TV shows even when they're muted,
For any lip reading challenge, I'm well suited.
And I understand folks even when they mumble,
Mispronounce, have a foreign accent, or fumble.

How we speak doesn't really matter, words or signs,
Just that we listen with open minds, all the time.
Because at the end of the day, as Zoe says,
'We are all unique just like everyone else is!'"

Then, Ursula shared a piece of her code,
With the girls to take with them on the road.
She explained to them that saying goodbye,
Is the same in her code and had them try.

179

Valerie never won a single thing,
Even though she tried to win everything.
She would enter every contest of skill,
Saying, "I'll win one day, one day I will."

She knew that winning wasn't the name of the game,
But she constantly made the effort just the same.
She tried sports and new skills without a single win,
But she knew she'd find something she could excel in.

And with each of her lost competitions,
Valerie gained fuel for her ambitions.
They pushed her to be better, try harder,
To practice more, and push herself farther.

Valerie was walking to school one day,
When she saw a flyer across the way.
It was an ad for a competition,
In mini golf; she had her new mission.

She made a copy of the sign-up sheet,
To see if anyone else would compete.
Her friends at school thought it looked like a blast,
Valerie signed up her entire class!

Finally, the day of the contest had arrived,
There were so many kids, Valerie was surprised.
Taking a deep breath, Valerie paused for a thought,
"Maybe today will be the day I win; why not?"

Even though she had only played golf once before.
She swung confidently at hole one; the ball soared!
On hole two, she had some trouble with the sand trap,
At hole three, Valerie's golf club abruptly snapped!
But by hole five, she had gotten into the groove,
She had perfected her stance and her swing was smooth!

Six holes in, the competition was tight,
But Valerie started swinging just right.
She scored a birdie on hole number eight.
With one hole to go, she was doing great!
"Yay! Go Valerie!", her friends loudly cheered.
She turned the corner, the last hole appeared.

It was the wackiest thing she had ever seen,
With curves, a windmill, and a teeter-totter beam.

Valerie took a deep breath, and lowered her head,
She knew that her friend, Quinn, was just two strokes ahead.
If she could hit the ball to the right of the crane,
Past the bouncing clown, and over the wooden train,
Then her ball should end up pretty close to the goal,
At the end of the course, to the right of the hole.

185

Quinn got to go first; she was as cool as ever,
First stoke, her ball flew; it couldn't have been better.
Second stroke, up and down the big teeter-totter.
Third stroke, in and out the windmill, past the water.
Fourth stroke, past the clown, the ball traveled very far,
Last stroke, it went up over the train; Quinn made par.

To win, Valerie had to make it in two strokes,
Her friends were loudly cheering her on with high hopes.
She turned to the crowd; "I'll do my best," she beckoned.
She was just happy to be sitting in second.
To be victorious, she just had to beat Quinn,
The really quick learner who, somehow, always wins.

Valerie closed her eyes and swung, "Here goes nothing!"
She hit the ball hard, her adrenaline rushing.
Around the curves, her ball seemed to grow wings and fly,
Up and over the obstacles, it rushed right by!

186

And then, Valerie's ball kept on going,
Through the windmill, it didn't start slowing.

Past the clown and train, she was nearly done,
PLUNK! Valerie got her first hole in one!

Valerie was sure that she was dreaming,
Everyone started cheering and screaming.
Quinn ran over shouting "Look what you've done!
Oh my goodness, Valerie, you have won!"

That day Valerie was victorious.
She was on top, and it was glorious.
She felt so proud; she couldn't stop blushing,
At the cheers, and beating Quinn at something.

Valerie told everyone that day that her win,
Was thanks to the persistence she put in.
She didn't let a fear of failing make her frown,
And insisted "failures should never slow us down.
They are simply a first attempt to teach us how,
To be better and stronger, right here and right now."

Everybody loved taking to Winnie,
She was bright, cheerful, and always witty.
She also had an incredible knack,
For giving thoughtful and honest feedback.

If you had a problem, Winnie was there,
With an ear to lend and a hug to share.
She listened and she heard before she spoke,
And could tell when you needed a good joke.

Just last week, when Winnie was with her friends,
Chatting at recess about odds and ends,
Noa mentioned her disappointment when,
She didn't make the bowling league again.

"Every time I try out, I get a no,"
Noa told her circle of friends with woe.
"I love bowling and I just want to scream,
I don't know why I never make the team."

Winnie responded, "You don't need the league to play.
Why don't we start our own team at the school, today?"
"Lots of us love bowling," Winnie continued on,
"We can put it together; I'll help liaison.

You know, if there's something you truly love doing,
You should never stop at no, just keep pursuing.
Because we are the ones who make our dreams come true,
Not other people; in the end it's up to you."

Noa smiled at Winnie, "That's a great idea,
We could use the alley by the pizzeria!"
And that's how the Alley Cats bowling team was born,
The newest bowling league this side of the seashore.

Later, Winnie saw Ophelia looking glum,
in the cafeteria, picking at some crumbs.
Winnie asked her "What's up?" as she pulled up a chair,
"Not much," she replied as she stared off to nowhere.

After a few minutes and hesitating twice,
Ophelia asked, "Maybe you have some advice?"
She went on to tell Winnie all about a cat,
That had been missing for weeks, maybe more than that.
She had looked, asked around, and was starting to doubt,
Her ability to figure anything out.
"I've asked everyone," Ophelia repeated,
"No one has seen anything, I feel defeated."

Winnie thought for a minute, then she said,
"I can hear your disappointment and dread.
It sounds like the worries of yesterday,
Are taking away from your joy today.
When that happens, I find that it is best,
To take a moment away, and to rest.

Taking a break is really effective,
For seeing things in a new perspective.
Then go back to it on a fresh, new day,
To see if you missed something on the way."

The next day, Ophelia came running, arms wide,
Heading for Winnie, hugging her tight, side to side.
"Your wise words did the trick, I found the missing cat!
I took your advice; it was as easy as that!"

That weekend was the first game for the Alley Cats,
Noa had arranged for matching jerseys and hats.
When Winnie received hers, she was surprised to see,
"Winnie the Wise" written across the back in green.

All of the girls felt happy and were filled with glee,
Because they were part of the brand new bowling league.
Thanks to Winnie's wise advice, they had created,
A new team where inclusion was cultivated.

Her words for Ophelia were also just right,
As the lost cat's owner catered every game night.

The first night of bowling, the Alley Cats had fun,
Though Noa was upset with her score of just one.
Winnie approached Noa with more wise words to say,
"I guess the bowling pins have gone on strike today!"

195

Xena the Xenial

Xena was appropriately named, so they say,
As she was xenial, welcoming in her ways.
Everyone felt special when Xena was around,
Because she made time for everyone, the whole town.

Every week, Xena invited someone to come,
Join her for a fabulous tea party for fun.
At school, each friend would get so excited,
When they were the one to get invited.
One by one they got their invitation,
To join their friend Xena at a fun location.

The arranging was all Xena's doing,
She'd set the table, get the tea brewing.
Put out her finest cups and papery,
And pastries from the local bakery.

One week, Xena met Danielle at the racing track,
Where she had just won her first race, on the last lap!

Xena knew it was a place Danielle loved to be,
So she packed a picnic and went to hear and see,
About all the daring things Danielle loved to do.
The girls talked and laughed the entire afternoon.

Another time, Christina was the main feature,
At a party at the Museum of Nature.
Xena and Christina had a great time talking,
About everything science: gems to sleepwalking!

This week, Xena invited the school's new student,
Jasmine, to help her feel settled and included.
As Jasmine was new, Xena thought it sensible,
To have the party at home on her sectional.

That afternoon tea party, Xena learned so much,
That Jasmine loved clementines and raspberry punch,
She wanted to grow up to be a judge one day,
And had never been skiing or ridden a sleigh!

Jasmine learned a lot of things about Xena too,
Her most favorite place to go was the zoo.
She got her love of pastries from her mom,
She never left the house without lip balm.

201

But before the party came to a final close,
Jasmine had one more important query to pose.
She turned to Xena, her eyes wide with questioning;
"My dear new friend, how come you are so welcoming?"

Xena laughed, as she had heard this question before,
From her parents and friends and her neighbor next door.
She turned to Jasmine with a quick, casual smile,
Then laughed saying "Sit back down, this may take a while.

I welcome everyone because I never know,
Where other people have been, or where they might go.
We have so much we can learn from one another,
But only if we can listen to each other.
This means taking the time, being intentional,
Even if my methods are... unconventional.

I think everyone is special in their own way,
and has something to offer each and every day.
I think remembering that makes us all more kind,
and hospitable to every person we find."

Jasmine smiled, "That is a good perspective to take,
It seems everyone makes the same silly mistake,
Of scurrying around and not stopping to see,
What we can all offer each other, you and me.

I have been feeling pretty lost in this new place,
And overwhelmed by every new building and face.
But after today, I feel better than ever,
Thanks for taking the time to invite me over."

That day, both of the girls left with a brand new friend,
And Xena resolved that her parties wouldn't end.
Because making time for others, she concluded,
Spread joy by making them feel special. Included.

Xena's tea parties continued all school-year long,
Until everyone had their chance to come along.
Week by week she carefully planned her schedule,
To host her tea parties where every guest is special.

Yuna the Young

Yuna was the youngest girl in her family,
A position of honor she held happily.
Except for when she tried to play with her sisters,
Then being the youngest was more of a blister.

Yuna always wanted to play with her siblings,
But they would ignore her, hurting Yuna's feelings.
When Yuna tagged along with them and made a fuss,
They would whine, "You are too little to play with us."

No matter Yuna's arguments or claims,
She was always excluded from their games.
But still Yuna asked, every single time,
In the hopes her sisters would change their minds.

One afternoon, Yuna heard her sisters playing,
But she couldn't quite make out what they were saying.
Yuna followed their voices, hoping to be part,
Of whatever fun things that were about to start.

She went upstairs to find marbles in a circle.
They were so beautiful, some sparkly, some purple.
There must have been two dozen, maybe even more,
They looked like little gems scattered over the floor.

Before she could ask, her sisters stood united,
And said, "You can't play with us, you weren't invited!
This game is for us older girls, you are too young,
We're sure you wouldn't understand it." Their words stung.

But this time, Yuna had had enough of their "no"s,
She began to speak, taking a defiant pose.

"How come I'm not too young to help you with your chores,
But I'm too young for every game you play outdoors?
I'm not too young when you ask me to sweep your room,
But too young to play games with you in your bedroom?

Why is it when I want to play,
You two always turn me away?"

208

"I know you both think I'm just a young, little girl,
But I'm good at things too, let me give it a whirl.
Maybe little is an advantage," she reasoned,
"Why don't you ever let me try?" Her voice weakened.

"Okay, fine!" Yuna's sisters finally gave in,
"But we're bigger than you, so we're going to win.
And when you do lose we don't want to hear crying."
Yuna nodded, :I'm just happy to be trying."

On the first play, her oldest sister overshot,
And the marble rolled in to a dark, far-off spot.
Because she played her turn like such an aggressor,
The marble ended up lodged under the dresser.

Her sister went over to retrieve it but found,
She couldn't fit between the dresser and the ground.
So Yuna's middle sister went over to try,
But the fit was too tight; she pinched her arm and cried.

When both of Yuna's sisters turned to her, she knew,
It was time to shine; little hands to the rescue!

Her hand fit under the dresser with ease,
She didn't even have to try to squeeze.
Both of her sisters cheered, and Yuna grinned,
Today, the littlest brought home the win!

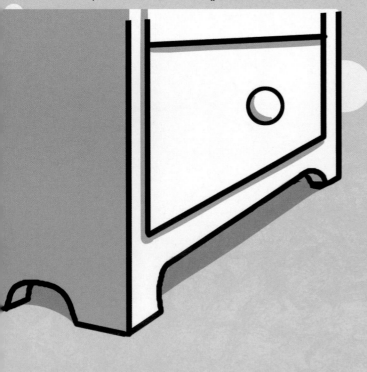

That day, her sisters realized young isn't bad,
In fact, it can come with some benefits to add.
They learned that being young can be beneficial,
And no longer used it as grounds for dismissal.

The next time they heard that Yuna wanted to play,
Her two sisters did not blindly turn her away.
Yuna had finally successfully managed,
To convince them that young can be an advantage.

Zoe did everything with enthusiasm,
Even her daily chores, which is hard to fathom!
Because she knew everything had the potential,
To evolve into something more consequential.

With every opportunity Zoe explored,
There came the guarantee that she would not be bored.
"Expect the unexpected," she would always say,
It was how Zoe approached every single day.

Her enthusiastic mindset was contagious,
Even though it sometimes seemed a bit outrageous.

Last week, Zoe's friend Gina was talking,
But before too long, she began balking.
Over a new circus exhibition,
By the bay; the girls were to audition.

"I'll try juggling, but nothing else," Gina said,
"I really don't want to fall on top of my head!
The tightrope looks too hard, the trapeze too scary,
Maybe I'll stay home that day," Gina looked wary.

"No way!" Zoe said jumping to her feet,
"Circus acts sound amazing! What a treat!"

"I don't know..." Gina said, looking away.
Then Zoe piped in, "We'll have a hay-day!
How often do you we get to fly from a trapeze?
Or walk on a tightrope? Nothing great comes with ease.
I will be there to support you, it will be fun.
We are all beginners, no one knows how it's done."

Zoe could tell Gina was getting excited,
But still scared of falling, getting hurt, or slighted.
Zoe went on, "If we never try something new,
How can we possibly know how much we can do?
And together, we can accomplish so much more,
Because we can pick each other up off the floor."

Gina agreed. They met up the next day,
For the circus auditions by the bay.

Zoe tried the tightrope first, and fell quite a bit,
For each fall she rose again and at last crossed it.
With Zoe cheering her, Gina gave it a try,
It seemed to take her no effort, she just flew by.

"You are a natural," Zoe started shouting,
"And to think that you were seriously doubting!"

As Gina came down from the tightrope with a smile,
She turned to ask Zoe, "Can we stay here a while?
I'm having a blast, and that really was a breeze,
Who knows, I might also be good at the trapeze!"

Zoe and Gina stayed all afternoon,
Trying everything that balanced and zoomed.
They were supportive at every attempt,
Fail or succeed, no matter how it went.

That day, Gina displayed such bravery and flair,
And she knew it was Zoe who'd gotten her there.
By encouraging her, Zoe helped Gina learn,
Excitement is often waiting around each turn,
And that she should face it head on, rather than doubt,
Whether she should try something new or just miss out.

After a day of fun, Gina turned to her friend,
And said, "Thanks for suggesting we come this weekend."
Zoe smiled and said, "Wasn't it so much better,
Trying something new and exciting together?"

That day, Gina gave the best tightrope audition,
And was awarded a guest circus position!
The next Saturday, Gina was asked to perform,
She crossed the tightrope with ease, she had perfect form.

Zoe found Gina after her circus debut,
Beaming with pride that Gina had tried something new.
The girls hugged, and then Zoe whispered in her ear,
So softly that only she and Gina could hear:

"When you are zealous, nothing is boring,
Even scary things are worth exploring.
Combined with the support of caring friends,
Everything is possible in the end!"

The fictional characters in childhood stories are some of our earliest teachers. We learn a range of things through the observation of these symbolic models, such as what is right and wrong, a desirable and undesirable behavior, gender roles, norms, stereotypes, and more. The role of models is particularly influential in childhood as it can have a long lasting impact on intellectual, social, emotional and moral development.[1,2,3] This is why it is critical to have stories that move beyond the belief that female characters are best suited as damsels in distress or need superpowers to be successful.

Pragmatic Princess not only changes the narrative to one of self-reliance, but does so with the power of science behind it. I drew heavily on my experience as a research psychologist to create stories that are fun and entertaining while also maximizing learning opportunities. This was done by carefully choosing the story length and structure, creating narratives that reflect the challenges and lessons of childhood, and developing a diverse cast of characters.

Story Length

A general rule of thumb is children's picture books should be between 500 and 1000 words. This length is short enough to hold the attention of the younger pre-readers but long enough to tell a fully fleshed out story. With this in mind, each story in the Pragmatic Princess was crafted to be between 450 and 650 words. This length also allows for multiple stories in the compilation to be read in a single session for the older readers.

Rhyming Scheme

Books that rhyme are fun to read because of their natural, song-like rhythm. They can also make the content easier to memorize for younger children, which can help transition them in to the pre-reading stage of development. This is an important milestone as it helps build confidence for reading and interest to further engage with reading. Rhyming is also an important part of reading success and it has also been found to encourage the development of writing skills.[4,5]

Diverse characters

It was important that the characters of Pragmatic Princess were diverse: all shapes and colors, many different backgrounds, with various abilities and disabilities, and from traditional and nontraditional families. It is important for literature to reflect our daily lives so readers can relate to the characters. The diverse cast also maximizes the learning opportunities within each story, as people are more likely to emulate role models of the same sex, ethnicity, and same skill level of any particular activity.[6,7,8]

To Lizzie Huxley-Jones and Claire Bogen: Thank you for all of your advice and feedback about this publishing journey.

To Billie Joe Armstrong, Mike Dirnt, and Tre Cool: In my life, every major milestone has been inexorably tied to your music. Thank you for providing the soundtrack to my life, including this publishing journey.

To Randall Hampton: I could not have asked for a better person to share this journey with. In addition to being an incredible illustrator, you are a wonderful friend. Over the last year, you have transformed my thoughts and ideas into something more than I could have ever dreamed. Thank you for your partnership.

Special thanks to Team Comfort and Adam: Melena Salinas, Kaitlynne Heyworth, Dylan Klingler, Alyssa Aman, Drew Norman, Alexis Kole, Jordan Vohel, Rae Barrett, Rya Emerick and Isaac Bergmann, for help with color seperation.

Last, but certainly not least, I would like to thank the castle builders who helped inspire the development of these characters and stories: Kristen Bell, Mayim Bialik, Farah Bullara, Kelli Butler, Ruby Cannon, Gwendoline Christie, Bella Davis, Katina Davis, Felicia Day, Ellen DeGeneres, Christina Delgado, Tanya DePass, Lady Gaga, Emma Gonzalez, Noah Hollis, Rachel Hollis, Gina Humphries, Paige King, Lucy Lawless, Jenny Lawson, Lisa Ling, Zoe London, Danica McKellar, Busy Philipps, Valerie Riha, Clea Shearer, Taylor Swift, Eliana Taylor-Redwood, Joanna Teplin, Jasmine Waters, Serena Williams, Reese Witherspoon, and Oprah Winfrey.

Through your words and actions you have shown the world that "happily ever after" does not come from luck or magic but from persistence and hard work. Thank you for paving the road for a new generation of castle builders and showing us that we all have the capability to write our own happy endings and build our own castles.